GROSSET & DUNLAP
Published by the Penguin Group
Penguin Group (USA) Inc., 375 Hudson Street, New York, New York 10014, USA
Penguin Group (Canada), 90 Eglinton Avenue East, Suite 700,
Toronto, Ontario M4P 2Y3, Canada
(a division of Pearson Penguin Canada Inc.)
Penguin Books Ltd., 80 Strand, London WC2R 0RL, England
Penguin Group Ireland, 25 St. Stephen's Green, Dublin 2, Ireland
(a division of Penguin Books Ltd.)
Penguin Group (Australia), 250 Camberwell Road, Camberwell, Victoria 3124, Australia
(a division of Pearson Australia Group Pty. Ltd.)
Penguin Books India Pvt.Ltd.,11 Community Centre, Panchsheel Park,
New Delhi—110 017, India
Penguin Group (NZ), 67 Apollo Drive, Rosedale, North Shore 0632, New Zealand
(a division of Pearson New Zealand Ltd.)
Penguin Books (South Africa) (Pty.) Ltd., 24 Sturdee Avenue,
Rosebank, Johannesburg 2196, South Africa
Penguin Books Ltd., Registered Offices: 80 Strand, London WC2R 0RL, England

ISBN 978-0-448-45617-1   10 9 8 7 6 5 4 3 2 1

HiT entertainment

Angelina's Perfect Party

inspired by the classic children's book series by author Katharine Holabird and illustrator Helen Craig

Grosset & Dunlap
An Imprint of Penguin Group (USA) Inc.

Angelina loved her ballet teacher, Ms. Mimi. That's why she wanted to throw her a very special surprise birthday party! Angelina's friends Gracie and Viki wanted to help, too.

"The first thing we need for the party is a present!" Angelina said.

Viki held her piggy bank up to her ear. She shook it and listened to the coins rattling around inside.

"If we put all of our money together, we can buy something really nice," Viki said.

Angelina and her friends couldn't wait to find the perfect present to give to Ms. Mimi at their perfect surprise party!

Angelina's friend Marco wanted to help, too. But he didn't want to go shopping.

"Is it okay if I stay here while you go shopping?" Marco asked.

He was too busy working on a special song on his guitar. So far he had written the music, but not the words.

"Of course, Marco! And we'll help you with your song after we find Ms. Mimi's present," Angelina promised.

Angelina, Viki, and Gracie said good-bye to Marco and raced into town. Angelina knew exactly where to go for the perfect gift: the ballet shop!

The first thing the mouselings saw when they
arrived at the ballet shop was a beautiful pair of silver
ballet slippers. Angelina gasped. They were perfect!

Angelina turned to her friends. "We simply *must* get these for Ms. Mimi!" she shouted excitedly.

Everybody agreed.

Gracie grabbed Viki's hand and pulled her into the store. "Ms. Mimi's going to love them!" Gracie squealed. "Just wait here, Angelina! We'll be back in just a moment!"

But when Viki and Gracie walked out of the store a few minutes later, they were not carrying the shiny, new ballet slippers.

"We don't have enough money to buy the slippers," Gracie said sadly.

"Oh no!" Angelina cried. "But we need to get Ms. Mimi the perfect present to show her how much we love her!"

Suddenly Viki had an idea. She turned to her friends

with a smile on her face.

"The shopkeeper told us that the ballet slippers were made by hand," she said.

Angelina thought for a moment and smiled. She understood Viki's plan! "You're right, Viki! My mom has satin in her sewing basket . . . "

"Then we can make the slippers ourselves!" Angelina, Gracie, and Viki all shouted at the same time.

The mouselings rushed back to Angelina's house, eager to get to work. There was no time to lose! Angelina quickly gathered ribbons, silver satin, and thread to make the slippers.

"Now that we've almost finished Ms. Mimi's present, we need to check on the cake!" Angelina reminded her friends.

"*Ooo!*" Gracie squealed. "I hope it's really big!"

The mouselings ran downstairs to the kitchen. Angelina's mom had been working all morning on Ms. Mimi's cake.

Everyone gathered around the table to admire the cake. It had pink and white frosting and one candle on top.

"It's very pretty, but I think it needs to be bigger," Gracie said. "We need a humongous cake to go with our spectacular birthday present!"

"You're absolutely right, Gracie!" Angelina turned to Mrs. Mouseling. "Mom, can we use the muffins you made earlier to add another layer to Ms. Mimi's cake?"

Mrs. Mouseling laughed. "Sure, Angelina. Just be careful!"

Viki and Angelina began stuffing muffins into a cake tin while Gracie and Marco went upstairs to work on the ballet slippers.

But before long, Ms. Mimi's perfect cake had turned into a big mess! The muffins had made the cake uneven, and the icing was dripping everywhere. But there was even worse news . . .

Gracie came downstairs carrying one of the ballet slippers. She held it out to Angelina. There was a hole in the toe!

"We must have cut it by mistake," Gracie said sadly.

"Oh no! The cake looks awful, and our handmade slippers aren't much better," Angelina said.

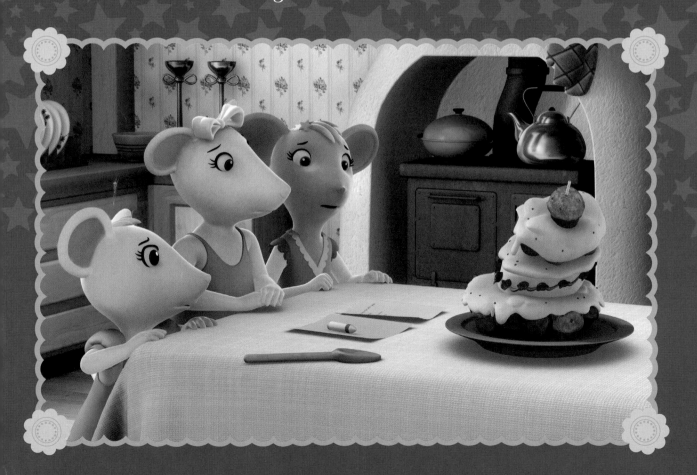

Gracie pointed to the clock on the wall. "There's no time to worry about that! We have to leave for the party in ten minutes."

While everyone cleaned up, Polly danced to Marco's new song, and Angelina made up words to go along with the music.

"Marco, this song reminds me of Ms. Mimi!" Angelina said. She sang her lyrics while Marco strummed. *"Here's a song for you, a song, la-la, a song for all the things you do!"*

Even though they still didn't have a present for Ms. Mimi, everyone was in a much better mood after listening to Marco and Angelina's song. Angelina hurried to Camembert Academy to decorate for the party. Marco and Polly left a little while later, carrying Ms. Mimi's lopsided birthday cake. But on the way to school, Marco sneezed and lost his grip on the cake. It fell to the ground with a big crash!

Angelina, Gracie, and Viki gasped when they saw Ms. Mimi's cake on the ground.

"Oh no!" Angelina groaned. "We don't have a present, I couldn't find any decorations, and now—no cake! How are we supposed to throw a party for Ms. Mimi?"

Polly reached into her bag and pulled out a muffin she had saved. She handed it to Angelina. "We could use my muffin as a cake," Polly suggested.

"Thanks, Polly!" Angelina thought for a minute. "Polly, what else is in that bag?" she asked.

Everyone watched as Polly pulled out crayons and drawing paper from her bag. This gave Angelina another idea. In no time, the mouselings had made party decorations from the daisies and ivy that they pulled from the ground. And they used Polly's supplies to draw a beautiful birthday card for Ms. Mimi.

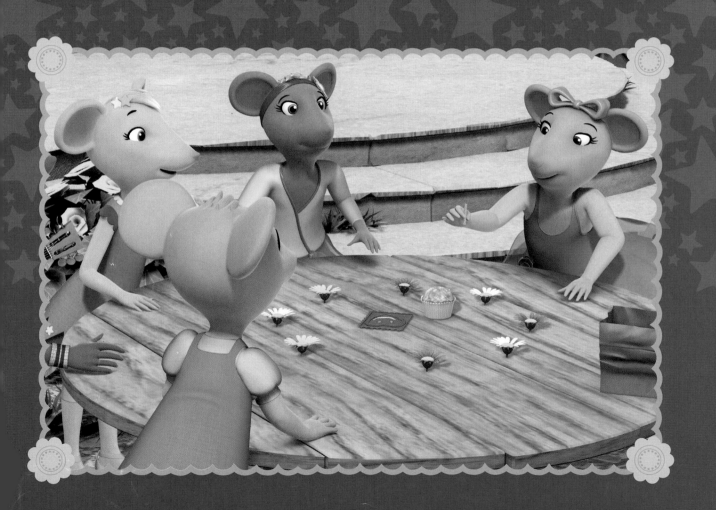

Just then, Ms. Mimi arrived. She looked around at all of the beautiful decorations. "Is someone having a party?" she asked.

Everyone stopped what they were doing and ran over to Ms. Mimi.

"*SURPRISE!*" they shouted all together.

Gracie handed Ms. Mimi her birthday card. Polly gave Ms. Mimi the muffin with the single candle on top. But there was one surprise left.

"We're sorry we couldn't buy you anything for your birthday, Ms. Mimi. But we do have something for you," Angelina said.

She gathered her friends together and began to whisper. Marco picked up his guitar and strummed a few chords.

The mouselings hurried up to the stage, including Alice, who had come to school for the party. Angelina, Viki, Gracie, and Alice began to sing while Marco played his guitar. Polly leaped, twirled, and jumped across the stage to the beat of the music.

"*Here's a song for you, a birthday song, for all the things you do! A jump! A leap! A twirl! A song to show we care,*" they sang together.

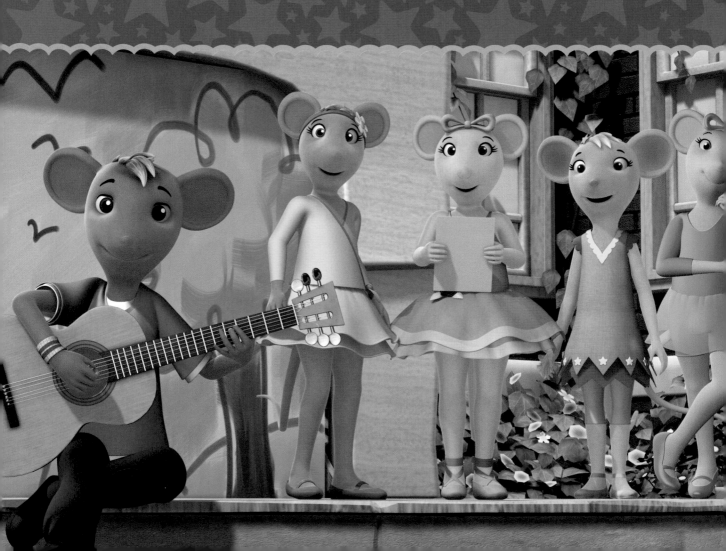

Ms. Mimi clapped her hands as Angelina and her friends finished their performance.

"That song is the most wonderful gift in the world. And you've given me another present, too," Ms. Mimi said. "This incredible celebration! To be really good, all a gift needs is to have lots of love in it."

Ms. Mimi gave everyone a great, big hug to thank them for all her wonderful gifts. Angelina smiled and hugged her friends and teacher tightly. It really was the most special birthday party she could have ever imagined!